for emma sophia price olsen - w.a.

A TEMPLAR BOOK

First published in the UK in 2003 by Templar Publishing,
an imprint of The Templar Company plc,
Pippbrook Mill, London Road, Dorking, Surrey, RH4 1JE, UK
www.templarco.co.uk

Distributed in the UK by Ragged Bears Ltd.,
Ragged Appleshaw, Andover, Hampshire, SP11 9HX

First edition

ISBN: 1-84011-599-8

Designed by Mike Jolley
Edited by Marcus Sedgwick

Printed in Belgium

The Dragon Machine

written by Helen Ward

illustrated by Wayne Anderson

templar publishing

george noticed
his first dragon on
a wet Thursday.

the more he looked, the more dragons he saw!

unseen, ignored and overlooked
the dragons went unnoticed...

...just like George.

Dragons perched on the telephone wires,

they sat amongst the dustbins.

They chased butterflies through the tulips.

They played havoc with the cat.

They sank the water lilies in the pond.

george fed them delicious stale biscuits and smelly cheese.

and then
the trouble began.

The dragons followed George everywhere.
George spent more and more of his time cleaning up
muddy footprints, tidying untidiness and saying sorry
for breaking things **he** had not broken.

George's dragons were becoming too troublesome
to stay unnoticed for much longer.

something had to be done.
George went in search of some advice.

The dragons
followed George to the library.

He consulted the Encyclopedia of Dragons.
There were dire warnings: never feed a dragon;
never let a dragon into your home... too late.
There were tragic tales of dragons discovered
and captured... too sad.

And there was a map of the place
where dragons belonged.

A great wilderness unnoticed
and overlooked and safe.
But George would have to
show them the way.

HERE BE
DRAGONS

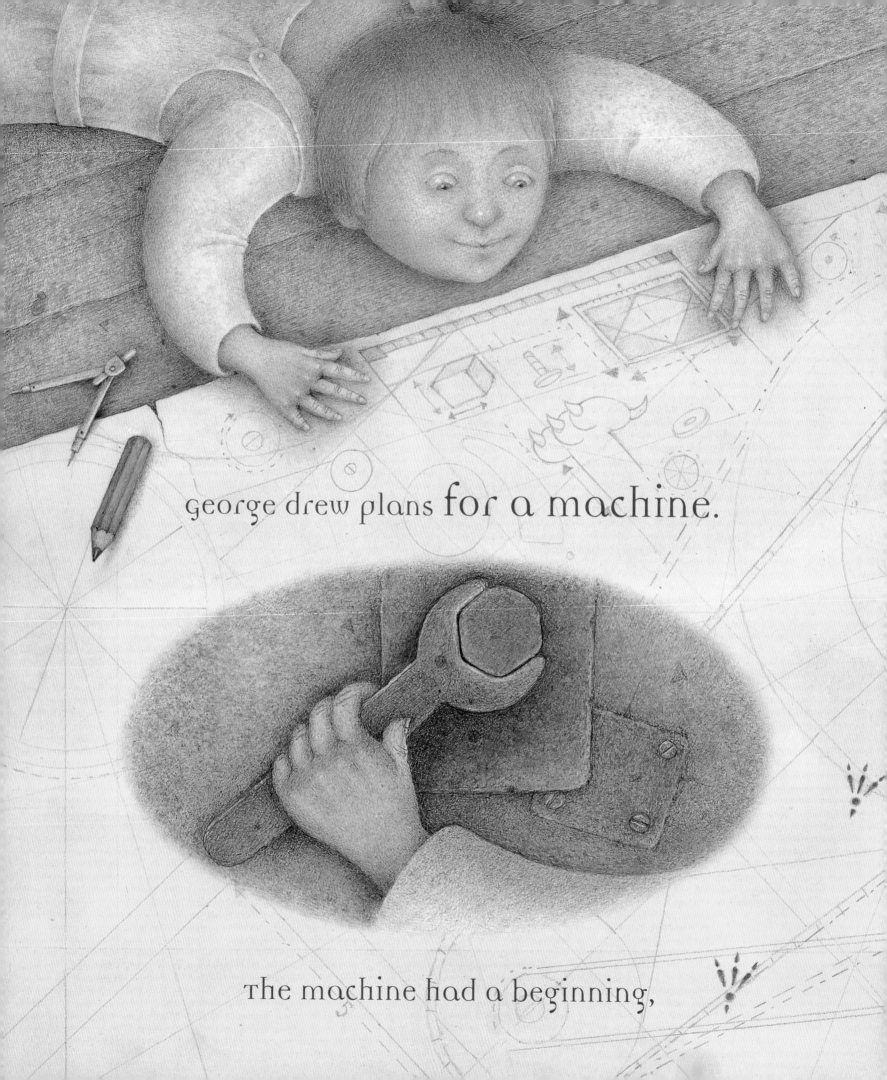

george drew plans for a machine.

the machine had a beginning,

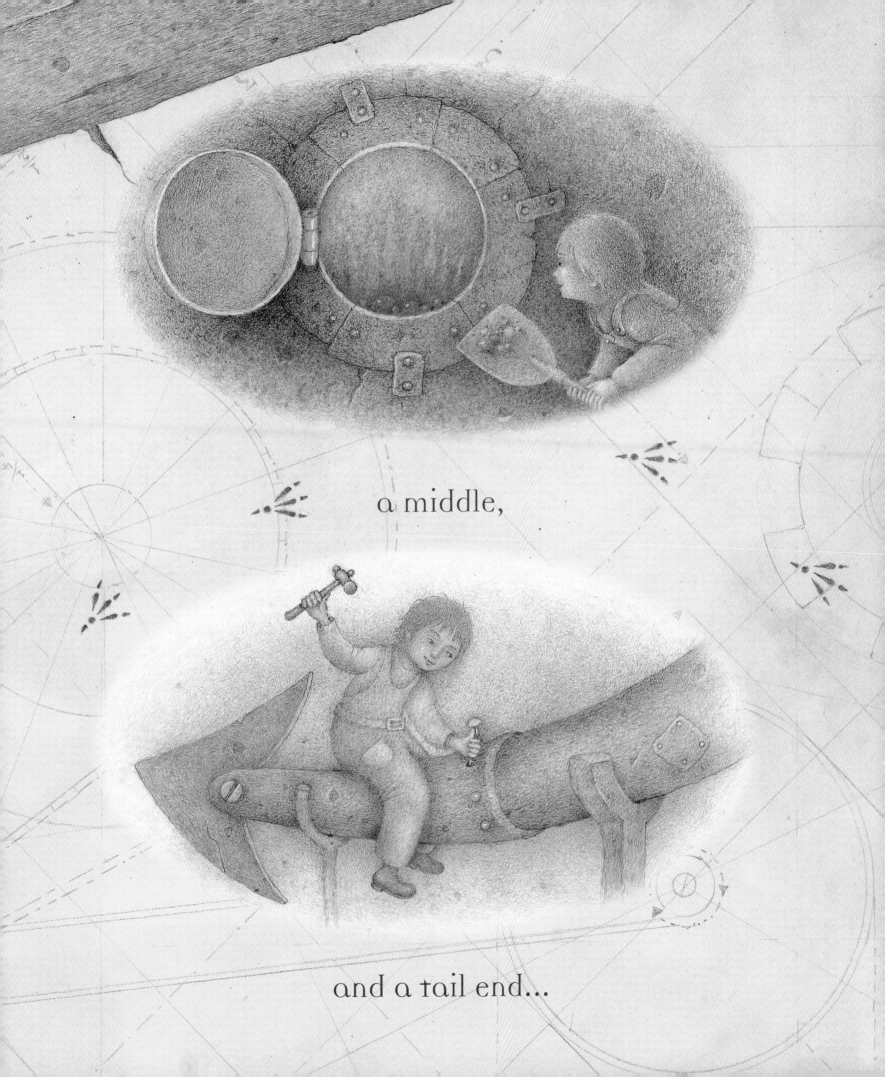

a middle,

and a tail end...

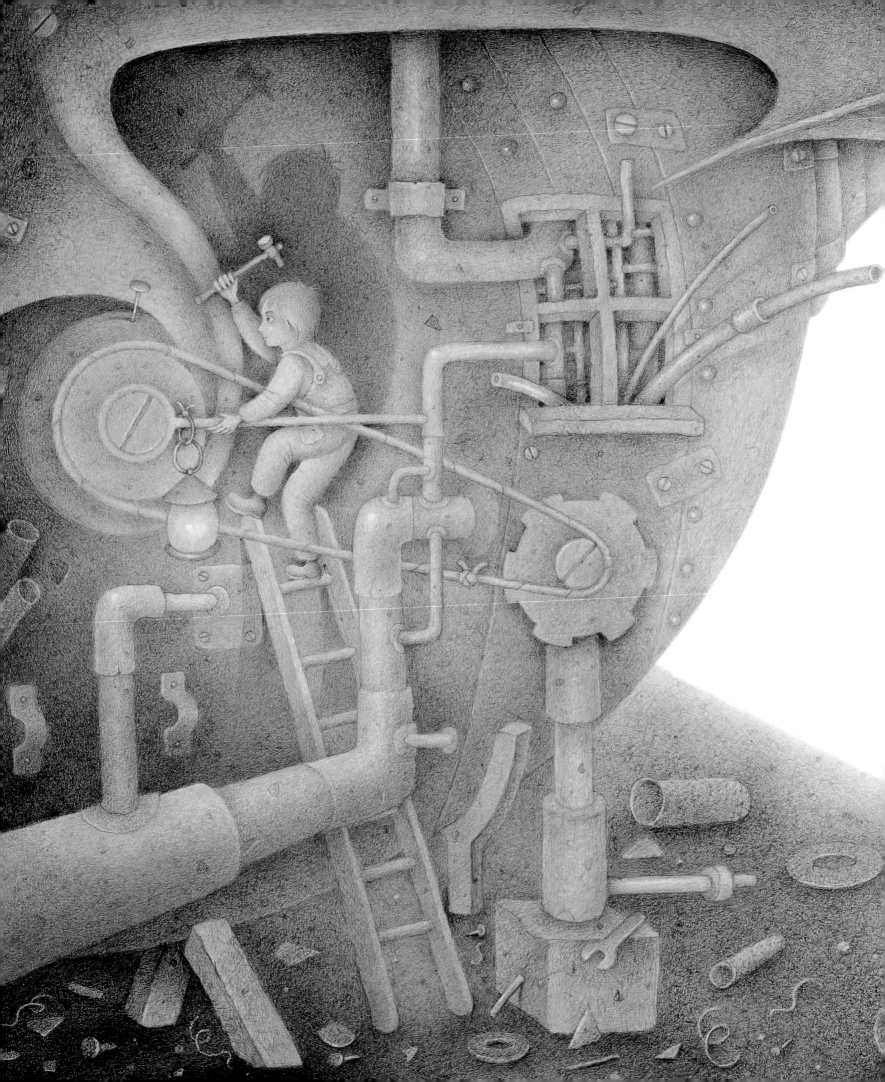

...an undercarriage,
and beautiful wings.

George hammered in the last nail.
He packed delicious stale biscuits and smelly cheese
and himself into the dragon machine.

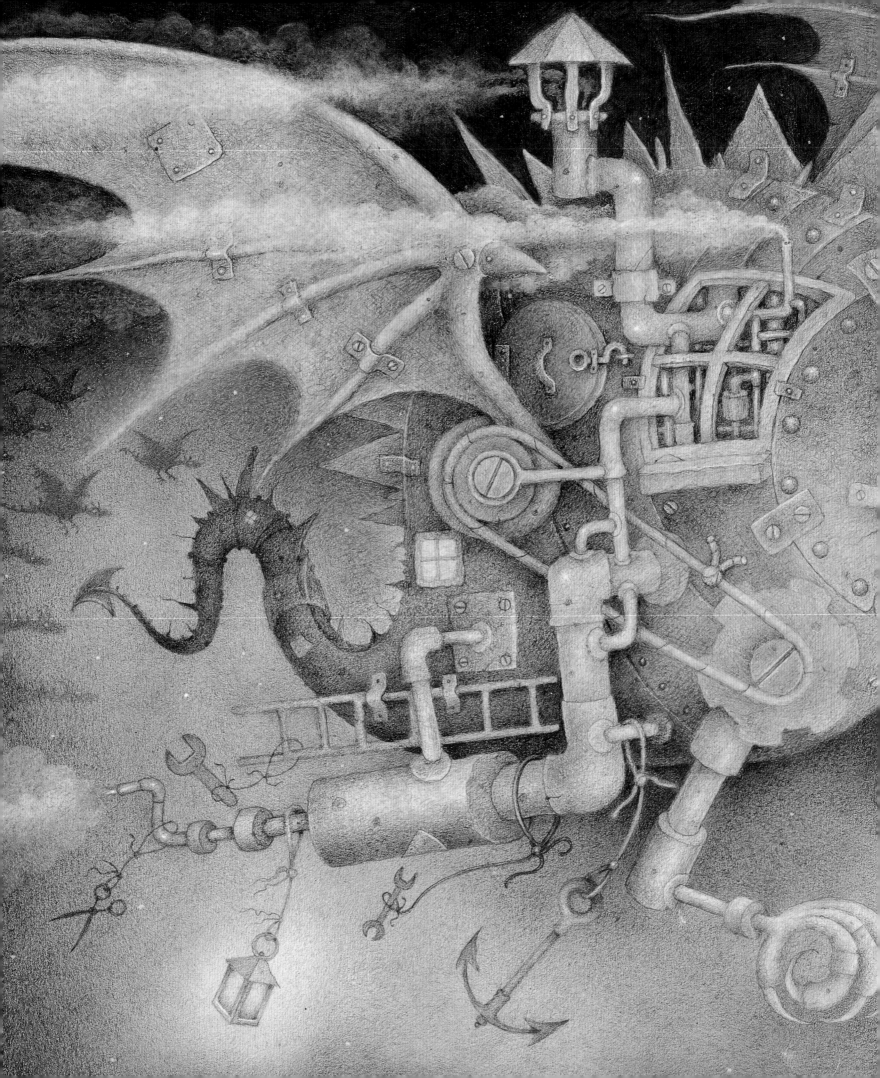

The machine lumbered, engine
ticking gently, into the night sky.

And the dragons followed.

The machine clicked
and whirred over the sleeping town.
It rattled and clunked
over the moonlit fields and woods.

The dragons followed.

It clattered and banged
and **crashed** into the great wilderness.

The dragons followed.

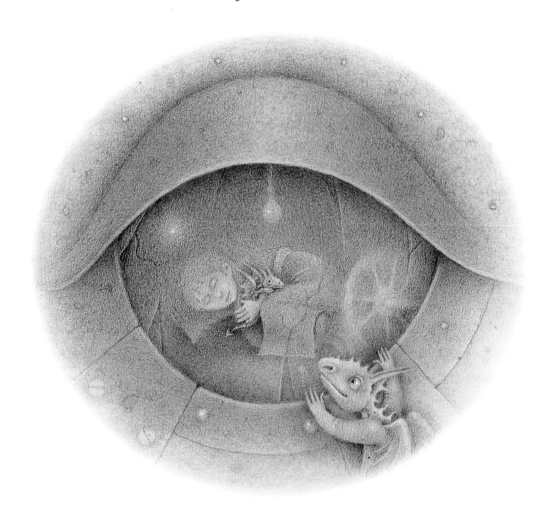

George was so tired he went to sleep
in the wreckage of his dragon machine.

By morning, all the dragons were gone.

There was an emptiness all around
and inside George.

And an emptiness at home where
george **should** have been.

They searched the town.
They searched the fields.
They ventured into the great wilderness
looking for george and found him among the
broken pieces of his dragon machine.

george and his dreams of dragons went home.

Everyone was pleased to see George,
and George was pleased to be back.
He no longer went unseen,
ignored and overlooked.

They made him a huge cake
to celebrate his return and gave
him a **dog** as a present.

nobody else noticed that it
wasn't a dog.